You Bet!

BY MARV ALINAS • ILLUSTRATED BY KATHLEEN PETELINSEK

We have not **met**.
My name is **Bret**.

I like my **jet**.

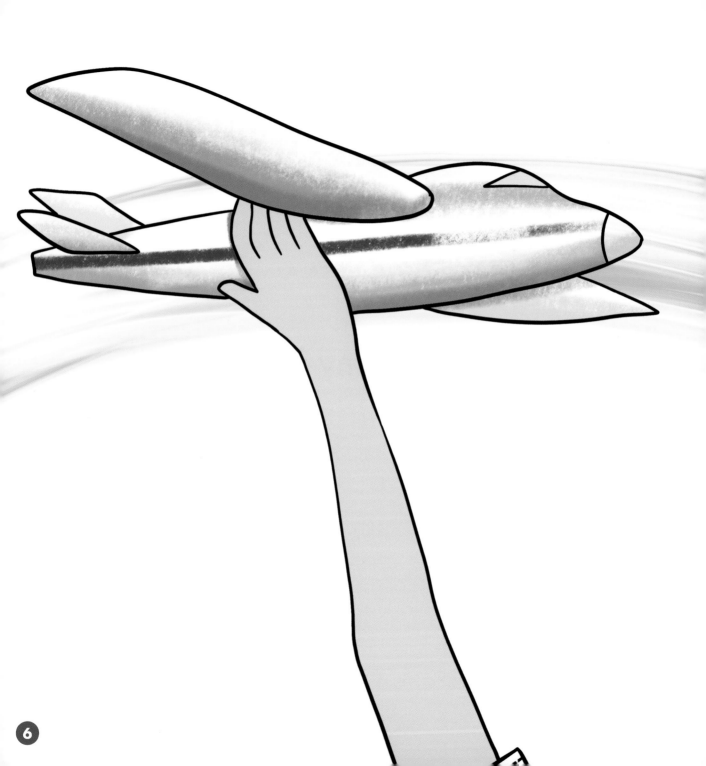

I can make my **jet** go high.

I can make my **jet** go low.

Do I like my **jet**?
You **bet**!

Now I will **get** my **net**.
Do I like my **net**?
You **bet**!

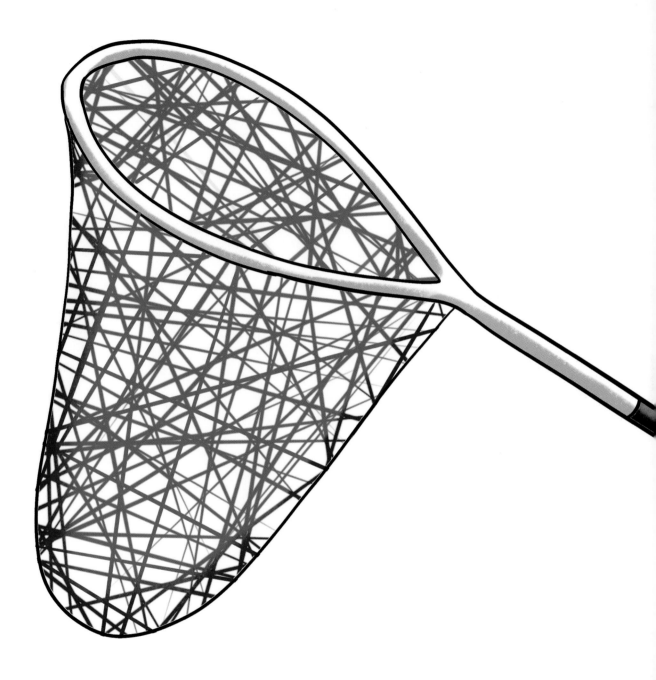

I find my **pet**.
Do I like my **pet**?
You **bet**!

I put my **net** on my **pet**.

My **pet** does
not like the **net**!

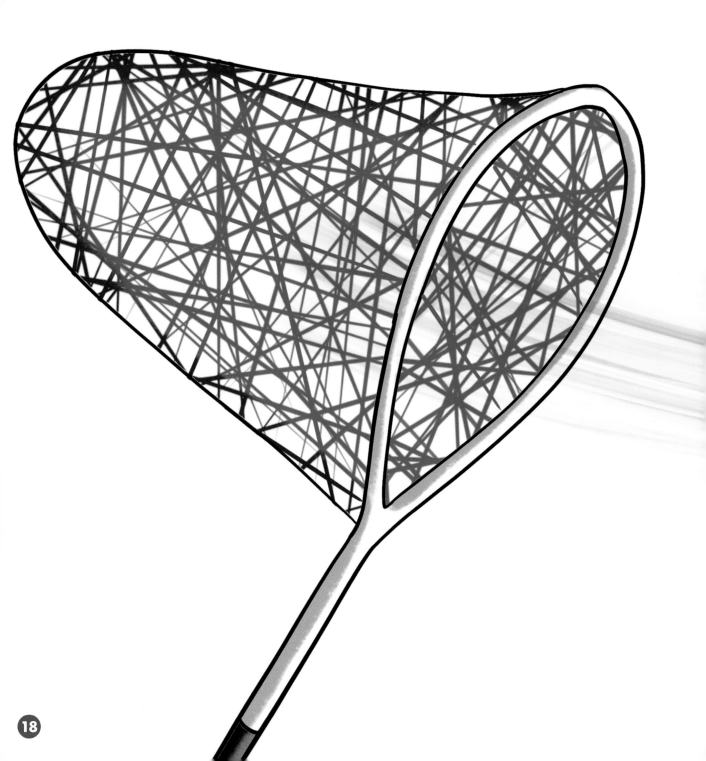

Do not **fret**, **pet**.
I will take off the **net**.

We will go play with the **jet**, **pet**!

Word List

b**et**	l**et**
Br**et**	m**et**
fr**et**	n**et**
g**et**	p**et**
j**et**	

Which Words Rhyme?

About the Author

Marv Alinas has written dozens of books for children. When she's not reading or writing, Marv enjoys spending time with her family and traveling to interesting places. Marv lives in Minnesota.

About the Illustrator

Kathleen Petelinsek has loved to draw since she was a child. Over the years, she has designed and illustrated hundreds of books for kids. She lives in Minnesota with her husband, two dogs, and cat.

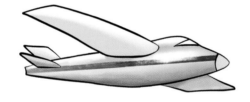

The **Child's World**®
childsworld.com

Published by The Child's World®
1980 Lookout Drive • Mankato, MN 56003-1705
800-599-READ • www.childsworld.com

ISBN Hardcover: 9781503827639
ISBN Paperback: 9781622434817
LCCN: 2018939257

Printed in the United States of America
PA02393